Blurb

A lone wolf, a mysterious partner, and a destiny that will change everything.

Erik is a private investigator living a life of exile, burdened by a werewolf curse he cannot control. Solitude is his sanctuary until Mira walks into his life, challenging his isolation and seeing the hero within him.

Working together, they discover that their connection and the dark magic plaguing Lycan-ridge are intrinsically linked. Erik's curse is the key, and breaking it is about more than just his freedom —it's about unlocking the town's supernatural past and forging a new future.

As an undeniable bond grows between them, a new prophecy emerges, hinting that their journey is far from over. He is the wolf, and she is the beacon. Together, they must face the shadows or risk losing not only their town but each other.

CURSE OF THE WOLF MOON

RUBY FOX

For those who find magic in full moons and solace in the howl of wolves.

Love
Ruby Fox x

This book has been written using US English, but the book's story is set in Australia. Some euphemisms that form part of the Australian spoken word may be used. If you would like further explanation, or to discuss Australia, please do not hesitate to contact the author. Contact details have been provided, for your convenience, at the end of this book.

CURSE OF THE
WOLF MOON

Chapter 1

Erik

THE CURSE WAS GOING to be the death of me, one way or another. But first, I had a cheating wife to catch. That's if I could keep my eyes off the rising full moon in the sky.

I glanced at the clock on the dashboard of my unmarked 1985 Ford Crown Victoria—10:07 p.m. Less than two hours until the transformation would begin, and the beast within me would take control. It would leave a trail of destruction and regret in its wake if I didn't make it to my dugout and lock myself in.

Yet, here I was, sitting in my car, on a stake out along the trendy Obsidian Avenue, all because

Marcus Holloway suspected his wife, Celine, wasn't faithful to him. The street was lined with chic boutiques, upscale restaurants, and luxury apartments, their neon signs and well-lit storefronts a stark contrast to the darkness that lurked within me.

How I wished I could've told Marcus where to stuff his request, but I needed the money. Ever since I left the force, I had to take whatever job came my way.

The almost five-figure paycheck Marcus promised could mean the end of these shit jobs, but only if I got proof of where Celine was going on these Friday nights. The problem was I wasn't sure whether Marcus wanted his wife to be having an affair or not. Either way, I was toast if I didn't deliver.

I shifted in my seat, the worn leather creaking beneath me as numbness spread across my backside. Celine should've come out of their fancy apartment building, the Moonstone Tower, by now. Its sleek, modern façade loomed over the street, the top floors disappearing into the misty night sky. Marcus had assured me she would be out by eight o'clock on the dot, based on when she'd been entering the alarm code.

Two hours I'd been waiting, and still no sign of her.

Dread knotted in my stomach.

What if I'd missed her?

The answer tore at my insides like my inner wolf was already pushing through my human form. It was a feeling I knew all too well, a curse that had haunted me for years. All because of a single moment of failure resulting in a night that changed everything.

Exiled from my pack and forced to leave the police force, I became a lone wolf haunted by my past mistakes. And since I couldn't control my transformations, I had to live a lonely life. Being a private investigator meant I could earn some money and help the underdogs, but it wouldn't ever stop the curse.

The nightlife was beginning to heat up around me, a steady stream of cars cruising down the avenue, their headlights reflecting off the rain-soaked pavement. I willed myself to be patient, but my inner wolf was keen to break this wait and come out early.

As the minutes ticked by, the pull of the curse grew stronger, my bones aching with the impending transformation. I couldn't afford to lose control, not when so much was at stake.

A flicker of movement caught my eye. A figure emerged from the shadows of the Moonstone

Tower, the click of high heels echoing in the night. Celine Holloway, dressed to kill in a form-fitting black dress and designer heels, was clearly on a mission.

She slipped into the back seat of a sleek black car, my heart pounding in my chest. This was it, the moment I'd been waiting for. I revved the engine of my Crown Vic, ready to follow her. The hunt was on, and I could only hope I'd remain in my human form long enough to see it through.

I tailed the car at a safe distance, my eyes never leaving the back of Celine's head. The city's nightlife blurred past my windows as we wound through the streets of Lycanridge, the cab driver oblivious to the predator following in their wake.

After a twenty-minute drive, I pulled up to a curb in a quieter part of town. Keeping my cover, I parked a short distance away. I watched as Celine stepped out, her silhouette illuminated by the lone streetlight overhead, her gaze sweeping before she settled further into the shadows of the street.

Celine's heels clicked on the concrete footpath, a slow rhythm out of place compared to my pulse. She paused at the rustic door, paint peeling off the wood, the streetlight above brightening the fading sign, '*The Whispering Tome.*'

The shop front was a relic from a bygone era

with large, dusty windows displaying ancient leather-bound books and strange, arcane artifacts. The building seemed to emanate an eerie energy as if the walls were imbued with the magic of the tomes within. The brickwork was old and crumbling in places, and the wrought-iron door handle was shaped like a coiled serpent, its eyes glinting in the moonlight.

She slipped inside, and I was left looking at the dusty windows as a worry for her life rose within. What business could she, a mundane, possibly have there?

If only I could ignore the paycheck and leave now. I needed the money, and I had to fight to stay in control. I could crack this case tonight, get the evidence of an affair, and report back to Marcus.

My wolf surged.

I checked my watch—eleven forty-five. The full moon was high in the sky, calling to my wolf, answering the call of the curse the witch had put on me as my punishment. It wouldn't be long before I would lose control.

But what if Celine needed my help?

I rushed out of my car, my heart pounding as I raced down the narrow, shadowy alley. The moonlight cast an eerie glow, creating dancing shadows that seemed to come alive with each hurried step.

The moon's pull was getting stronger, and I could feel my inner wolf stirring, clawing at the edges of my consciousness, ready to break free at the first sign of danger.

As I drew closer, I could feel the power thrumming through the air, a palpable force that set my teeth on edge and made my skin tingle. This was no ordinary bookshop. It was a gateway to the hidden world of the supernatural, a place where the secrets of magic and mystery were bought and sold.

I hesitated for a moment, my hand hovering over the serpent-shaped door handle. Did I really want to step into this world, to delve deeper into the darkness that had already consumed so much of my life?

The cold metal of the serpent's scales beneath my fingers sent a rush of trepidation through me as I grasped the handle. Then, with a sense of grim determination, I pushed open the door and stepped inside.

The musty scent of old books and ancient magic assailed my nostrils. The shop was cramped with towering bookshelves lining the walls and creating narrow, labyrinthine aisles. The shelves were packed with leather-bound books, their spines cracked and faded, and strange, arcane objects—crystals, talismans, and jars filled with mysterious substances—were scattered throughout the shop.

The dim, flickering light of old-fashioned gas lamps cast an eerie glow over the interior, creating dancing shadows that seemed to take on a life of their own. The air was thick with the hum of magic, a low, constant vibration that set my teeth on edge and made my wolf stir restlessly beneath my skin.

I wasn't familiar with the shop, but with the full moon high and my wolf so close to emerging, I knew this was a place for the supernaturals who lived in this town. But Celine was human, like her husband—or so I thought.

Had she discovered our world?

Deeper into the shop, I caught sight of Celine near the back, engaged in a heated discussion with a hooded figure and another man in a tweed jacket, perhaps the store owner. The man was tall and thin with a shock of white hair and a long, gray beard. He wore a black robe adorned with strange, silver symbols that seemed to shimmer and move in the flickering light.

I crept closer, straining to hear their conversation over my heart pounding. Celine's face was pale and drawn, her eyes wide with fear and desperation. The hooded figure loomed over her, their posture menacing, while the shop owner looked on with an expression of bleak resolve.

"I'll get the book for you," Celine pleaded, her voice trembling, "It was too dangerous today. You wouldn't want us to be all caught out?"

The hooded figure leaned in closer, their voice a sibilant whisper. "Are you losing your nerve?"

"No, I'm being careful, and you should do the same. The museum would know I took it. The trail would lead to you. Give me a few more days. I have staff covering different shifts, and it will be more difficult for authorities to notice *The Book of Forgotten Rituals* missing."

Was that it? I knew that title. It sent a coldness through me, and I shivered.

The book had been missing for decades, and it was the reason I was cursed. I should've destroyed it then, but I had been weak with the witches, gave in to their desires, and allowed them to complete the ritual to bring in the demon. I wouldn't make the mistake again.

A growl built in my throat, but I didn't know how long I could maintain control with the full moon's power coursing through my veins. But I had to get the book, and it wasn't here. It looked like I would be following Celine a lot more closely than her husband thought.

"Is someone there?" called out the man in the tweed jacket. "Didn't you read the close sign?"

I swore under my breath and edged backward, unsure of the powers these two supernaturals had. I couldn't fight if I were changing, but as I stepped back, hoping to slide into the shadows, I bumped into a tower of books, sending them tumbling with thumps that alerted them to where I was.

Fuck it all.

"You'll regret coming here…"

I didn't stay to hear anymore. I'd blown my cover, but worse, I knew it was midnight. I had to get out of there. My body contracted, a spasm of pain ripping through me. I'd ignored it too long. The change was coming.

It was me who was in danger now. I'd been too focused on Celine. I'd not allowed enough time to get back home to the safety of my basement.

Fur began to sprout along my arms and back. I had to find somewhere safe, where I could ride out the change without putting anyone else at risk.

I fled outside the store. Panic and rage surged through me, battling with the agony of the transformation. I couldn't let the wolf take control, not here, not now. With a herculean effort, I forced myself to my feet and staggered deeper into the alley, my vision blurring as the beast within me fought for dominance.

I managed to find an abandoned warehouse, its rusted metal door hanging off its hinges. I lurched inside, slamming the door shut behind me, but I knew the flimsy barrier wouldn't hold for long. The change was coming faster now, my muscles and sinews twisting and reforming beneath my skin.

Collapsing to the cold concrete floor, my worst fears were realized as the transformation consumed me. Through the haze of pain and the red mist of the wolf's rage, one thought crystallized in my mind. *I had failed* to control the beast within, and now, I feared I would fail to keep the innocent people of Lycanridge safe from the monster I had become.

The damage my wolf could do in one night could cost me everything.

Chapter 2

Mira

THE CURSOR BLINKED on the empty screen, taunting me with its steady rhythm. I'd been staring at it for what felt like hours, trying to find the right words to begin my article on the hidden supernatural underbelly of Lycanridge. As a journalist for the *Lycanridge Chronicle*, I'd covered my fair share of strange and inexplicable events, but this story was different. It was personal.

I leaned back in my chair, the old leather creaking under my weight, and rubbed my tired eyes. The office was quiet, save for the humming of the fluorescent lights and the occasional shuffling of papers from the few reporters working late. The clock on the wall read 11:58 p.m., a reminder of the relentless passage of time.

As a witch, I'd always been drawn to the mysterious and unknown. It was what had led me to pursue journalism in the first place—a desire to uncover the truth and shed light on the secrets that lurked in the shadows of our city. But even with my magical abilities, I'd barely scratched the surface of Lycanridge's supernatural world.

I glanced at the stack of files on my desk, each a tantalizing glimpse into a world most people never knew existed. I reveled in uncovering the dark underbelly of our supernatural society. Werewolf sightings, vampire attacks, and whispers of ancient curses—these were the stories that ignited my passion, tales that captivated the supernatural community and kept them hungry for more. These were the stories I knew could make my career if only I could find a way to bring them to light. But there was one story in particular that had consumed my thoughts for months—the legend of the *Book of Forgotten Rituals,* a powerful and dangerous book that was said to hold the key to unlocking the darkest secrets of the supernatural world.

I'd been chasing leads and gathering information, piecing together a puzzle that seemed to grow more complex with each passing day. I knew if I could find the book and uncover its secrets, I would finally have the proof I needed to expose the truth about Lycanridge's supernatural underworld. But the deeper I dug, the more I realized the story was far more dangerous than I had ever imagined.

More importantly, the book would help me to avenge my mother's death from those who wanted to cause chaos and practice dark magic. My fingers twirled on the heart-shaped locket that had been my mother's and held her photo around my neck.

As I sat in the dimly lit office, surrounded by the remnants of my research, a sense of anticipation coursed through my veins. I was on the verge of something big that could change everything. Little did I know, my chance to uncover the truth was about to come knocking at my door in the form of an anonymous tip that would lead me straight into the heart of the supernatural storm brewing in Lycanridge.

The shrill ring of my phone pierced the silence of the office, jolting me out of my thoughts. I glanced at the screen, expecting to see a familiar number, but instead, the words *'Unknown Caller'* flashed before my eyes.

Curiosity piqued. I answered the call.

"Mira Aldwood, Lycanridge Chronicle," I said,

my voice steady despite the flutter of excitement in my chest.

"I have a tip for you," a deep, distorted voice replied, sending a chill down my spine. "There's been a werewolf sighting in the abandoned warehouse on the corner of Elwood and Ninth. You might want to check it out."

Before I could respond, the line went dead, leaving me with a dial tone and a racing heart. I stared at the phone in my hand, my mind reeling with the implications of the anonymous tip. A werewolf sighting was rare, even in a city like Lycanridge, where the supernatural was more common than most people realized.

I knew I had to investigate, even if it meant venturing into the night alone. This could be the story I'd been waiting for. The one that would finally prove to my editors and the world that the supernatural was real and happening right under our noses. Plus, with any luck, it might bring me closer to finding the book.

I grabbed my coat and bag, stuffing my notepad and pen inside. I then checked my phone, making sure it was fully charged, and slipped it into my pocket. Despite the risk, I knew I couldn't let this opportunity pass me by. It was all too tempting.

I drove my beat-up Hyundai to the address

given in the tip-off. The cold night only added to my fear as I navigated the quiet city streets as most slept.

The abandoned warehouse loomed before me, its dilapidated exterior a testament to years of neglect. The windows were boarded up, and the metal doors were rusted and hanging off their hinges. I hesitated for a moment, my heart pounding in my chest as I contemplated the potential dangers that lay ahead.

But I couldn't turn back now. I'd come too far to let fear stop me from uncovering the truth. With a deep breath, I reached out with my magical senses, feeling the energy that pulsed through the building. It was dark and twisted, a swirling vortex of rage and pain that made my skin crawl.

With false confidence, I pushed open the door, wincing as it creaked on its hinges. The inside was pitch black, the only light coming from the moonbeams that filtered through the cracks in the boarded-up windows.

I summoned a small orb of light to guide my way, its soft glow illuminating the debris-strewn floor. As I picked my way through the rubble, I couldn't shake the feeling I was being watched. Every shadow seemed to hold a hidden threat, every sound a potential danger. I clutched my bag tighter, my other hand ready to cast a defensive spell at a moment's notice.

The scene of destruction that lay before me was like something out of a nightmare. The walls were covered in deep, jagged claw marks, the metal shredded like paper. Broken crates and shattered glass littered the floor, the remnants of a violent struggle that had taken place there.

My heart raced as I realized the true extent of my mistake. I had walked straight into the lair of a werewolf, a creature of immense power and ferocity. And now, I was trapped here with it.

Suddenly, a low growl echoed through the warehouse, sending a chill down my spine. I spun around, my orb of light flickering as my concentration wavered. And there, in the shadows, I saw it.

The werewolf was massive, its hulking form easily twice the size of a normal wolf. Its fur was deep, jet black, and matted with dirt and blood. Its eyes glowed a sickly yellow, fixed on me with a predatory intensity that made my blood run cold.

I stood frozen, my breath coming in short, panicked gasps as the creature stalked toward me, its lips pulled back, revealing razor-sharp fangs that gleamed in the moonlight. Power emanated from it, a raw, primal energy that threatened to overwhelm me.

For a moment, I was certain I was going to die here, torn apart by this monstrous creature. But then, something strange happened. The werewolf paused. Its head cocked to the side as if listening to something only it could hear. And then, to my shock, it began to change.

The wolf's body convulsed, its limbs twisting and contorting at unnatural angles. The sound of cracking bones filled the air, accompanied by the tearing of flesh as the creature's form began to shift. Fur receded into the skin, and the beast's muzzle shortened, reshaping itself into a human nose and mouth. The transformation was mesmerizing and grotesque, a reminder of the raw, primal power that lurked beneath the surface of the naked man before me, his muscular body covered in scars and tattoos.

He stared at me, his eyes still holding a hint of that predatory gleam. Was I going to be his next meal?

I swallowed hard, my mouth suddenly dry. I knew I should be running, but something held me in place. Something about this creature intrigued me. I couldn't let the tip-off go without investigating.

Why would someone want me to know about this werewolf? Especially this one who appeared out of control, unlike the other packed werewolves, who were contained.

There was a flame of chaos in the man's eyes that lured me in. I wanted to know why. They flashed with a feral intensity, and before I could blink, he lunged at me, his body morphing back into the monstrous form of the werewolf. I stumbled backward, my heart pounding in my throat as I felt the creature's hot breath on my face.

Instinctively, I threw up my hands, a burst of magical energy erupting from my fingertips. The spell slammed into the werewolf's chest, sending it sprawling backward into a pile of debris.

But the beast was far from defeated.

It sprung to its paws, shaking off the impact like it was nothing. Its eyes locked onto me once more, and I could see the rage and hunger burning within them. It crouched low, preparing to spring at me again.

My mind raced, searching for a spell that could stop the creature in its tracks. I'd learned countless incantations over the years, but in that moment of terror, they all seemed to flee from my grasp. And then, like a bolt of lightning, it hit me—a holding spell mixed with a cage spell. It was risky, one I'd never tried before, but it was my only chance.

I began to chant, the ancient words flowing

from my lips like a river. I could feel the magic building within me, a crackling energy that made my hair stand on end. The werewolf snarled, its muscles tensing as it prepared to attack.

And then, it leaped.

Time seemed to slow as the creature hurtled toward me, its jaws wide open, its razor-sharp teeth gleaming in the moonlight. I saw every detail of its face, every fleck of saliva that flew from its mouth as it snapped at my throat.

But just before it could reach me, the spell took hold.

A shimmering cage of energy materialized around the werewolf, slamming it to the ground midleap. The creature thrashed and howled, its claws scrabbling against the magical barrier, but it was no use. It was trapped, held fast by the power of my spell.

I staggered back, my heart racing, and my breath coming in ragged gasps. I couldn't believe it had worked. I'd never attempted such a complex spell before, let alone in the heat of battle with a rampaging werewolf.

But even as I marveled at my own power, I knew the danger was far from over. The werewolf was contained but for how long?

And what would happen when it broke free?

Chapter 3

———————————————

Mira

MY EYES NARROWED as I stepped closer to the cage, studying the creature within. The wolf snarled at me through the shimmering bars, his chest heaving with exertion.

"How long will you stay in wolf form?" I asked, my voice unusually calm despite the terror coursing through me. The sharp claws swung at me, and I flinched, remembering how close they had come to me before I'd cast the containment spell. If they had connected, I'd now be facing a life of turning each month.

I looked up into a gap in the warehouse's ceiling and glimpsed the full moon. I suppose we had a few hours left of him being in this form. But surely he could change back? The Moonlit Pack in this city prided itself on controlling its ability to transform.

Maybe this was my story, 'Lone Werewolf Threat to the Citizens of Lycanridge.' It could very well make the front page.

I took out my phone and snapped a few photos, causing the wolf to spring at the spell-electrified bars, teeth bared, growl menacing.

"Don't like that? Well, then I suggest you change back and start talking. Otherwise, you're tomorrow's front-page news."

He snarled back at me, long and deep, until my skin prickled.

"You're choice. If you don't turn back now, then I know you can't. And this… well, this is a story."

He continued to growl at me, his eyes a deep, flamed orange of hatred.

"I only want the truth."

I waited. Patience was something I'd learned on the job. There was no point trying to communicate with the wolf. I needed him to change back into a man. "I really don't want to harm you," I said, but my words didn't reach the wolf or indicate that the human man within was prepared to listen to me.

He wasn't changing back, and that sent shivers of excitement through me. This could be my chance to uncover a new story and get one step closer to the head journalist job.

My thoughts drifted back to the research I had been conducting on *The Book of Forgotten Rituals* before I received the anonymous tip about the wolf sighting. The ancient book had consumed my waking hours, a mystery that promised my mother's death.

But now, sitting here in the presence of this wild, untamed creature, I found myself torn. The wolf's appearance in the city was highly unusual, a break from the strict control and secrecy that the werewolf packs were known for. Clearly, this wolf was far from in control of its animal nature, a danger to itself and others.

As the full moon began to sink in the sky, I noticed a change in the wolf. The pain in its eyes reflected back at me, a mixture of agony and exhaustion.

The wolf was still caged, trapped by the spell I had cast for my own protection. I fumbled for my phone, eager to capture this moment on film, not wanting to miss a single detail.

Suddenly, the wolf lunged at the cage, throwing its body against the bars with a sickening thud. It ignored the painful zaps from the spell, its eyes wild with desperation. I gasped and stumbled backward, my heart pounding in my chest.

Would the spell hold against such a ferocious onslaught?

To my relief, the cage remained intact, the spell holding strong. But in my haste to retreat, I had dropped my phone. It lay on the ground, submerged in a puddle of filthy water. "Fuck," I muttered, gingerly picking up the device with two fingers, not wanting to touch the grime it had landed in. Gray water dripped from the bottom, and the smashed cover taunted me. I tried to turn it on, but the screen remained dark.

"This is your fault," I grumbled, juggling to retrieve a hanky from my bag to wipe down the phone.

The wolf, now calm, stared back at me with a smug expression on its face as if it knew the chaos it had caused. And then, the transformation began.

As the last remnants of the wolf melted away, I found myself staring at a handsome, rugged, stubbled face. The man's muscular body was covered in a sheen of sweat, his chest heaving with exertion. He looked up at me, his eyes still holding a hint of the wolf's intensity but now tinged with a exhaustion and confusion. Something stirred within me, and I fought to push down the desire building within me.

"Who are you?" he asked, his voice hoarse and strained.

I swallowed hard, my mind reeling with the implications of what I had just witnessed. I knew I should be afraid and turn and run as far away from this man as possible. But something held me in place, a burning curiosity that demanded answers to the questions that swirled in my mind.

I took a moment to study the man before me, taking in his rugged, handsome features. His dark hair was tousled, and his beard was unkempt, but it only added to his raw, masculine appeal. His eyes, a deep brown, seemed to hold a depth of pain and secrets I couldn't begin to understand. And he was naked. I quickly raised my eyes to meet his, heat rushing to my cheeks.

"I'm Mira Aldwood," I said, my voice trembling slightly, echoing in the vast, empty space of the abandoned warehouse. The air was thick with the musty smell of decay and neglect, and the only light came from the pale moonbeams filtering through the grimy windows.

"The bloody nosy journo," he said gruffly. His voice was deep and rough, like gravel, and it sent a shiver down my spine.

"I'll take that as a good thing you've heard of me."

"Why are you here? Was it to do with Celine? The book?"

My skin prickled. Could he be after the same book as me? That was a huge leap, and I needed to fact-check.

"What book? And who is Celine?"

"Never mind. Why are you here?"

"Hot tip-off." Somewhere in the distance, I heard the skittering of rats, and the faint drip of water echoed in the cavernous space.

"You have some enemies then?"

"Maybe. It was probably Celine or the book-store owner."

"Giving you over to the police as a wolf out of control. I must say, this is a good story for me."

"Don't print it, please." He had desperation in his voice, a raw vulnerability that tugged at something deep inside me, but I couldn't let it sway me.

I was a journalist, and I owed him nothing. This was the icing on the cake for my story. "Why not? You are a wolf who can't control your change. The citizens of Lycanridge deserve to know you are a threat."

"I'm not a threat, and it's not my fault."

I risked stepping close to the magical bars, protecting me from him. The air was thick with the pungent scent of wet fur and something else, something darker and more primal. It was the smell of a story that would give me the promotion I desperately wanted, the acrid tang of ambition mingling with the coppery scent of danger. "Why isn't it your fault?"

"I'm cursed."

Even better. A cursed wolf living in Lycanridge that no one knew about, one that could bring terror and chaos and death. My pulse quickened, the blood rushing in my ears like a distant drumbeat. The thrill of the hunt was upon me, and I could feel every nerve in my body thrumming with anticipation.

"What did this little puppy do to be cursed?"

He glared at me, his eyes flashing with a feral intensity that made my breath catch in my throat. "Nothing."

"Of course, you did nothing. Innocent, were you?"

"No. But if I tell you, promise me you won't print the story."

"I can't do that." The words felt heavy on my tongue, a bitter admission of defeat. I looked into his eyes and saw a sadness that seemed to wrap around my heart, tugging at the strings of my compassion. The moonlight filtering through the grimy windows cast shadows across his face, highlighting the sharp angles of his cheekbones and the dark hollows of his eyes.

"Why not? Forget about whatever promotion you think you'll get. I'm bad news of the worst kind."

Suddenly, recognition dawned on me, a cold shiver running down my spine. "You're the lieutenant, aren't you? Erik Talbot. Everyone was shocked about your resignation from the force and then your disappearance."

"I am. Please, this isn't the story you think it is. You'll risk your own life." His voice was low and urgent, barely audible over the distant drip of water echoing in the cavernous space. The raw edge of fear made my skin prickle with unease.

"It's why I'm a journalist. I can't help risking my life. And everyone will love to read what has happened to the lieutenant." I swallowed hard, my mouth suddenly dry as I realized the gravity of the situation I had stumbled into. This wasn't just another story or another chance at a promotion. This was something much bigger, much darker, and infinitely more dangerous.

"You won't be able to write it if you're dead."

"I don't plan on dying. Now, tell me." I scrambled in my handbag to get out my pen and notepad since my phone was now toast.

"No. Hang me out to dry then, tear apart what little good I might be doing, but I'll only tell you if you promise me."

The determination in his eyes was unmistakable. He no longer cared about his own life. Maybe I could hear him out and publish the story later, much later, then cash in on this wonderful timing and great tip-off.

"Fine, tell me." The words tumbled out of my mouth, and I couldn't believe I agreed to this. I never gave an inch, but something about this man warmed my heart, removing the cold walls I'd erected for being a journalist.

"Blood promise." He leaned forward, his face so close to the magical bars zapping with my magic, their light pushing away some of the shadows around us.

"Fuck you." No way was I doing that. It meant I could never tell his story, ever.

"Fine." He stepped back from the bars and turned away. "Your funeral."

"The only funeral happening is yours."

"What are you going to do with me now?" He

hung his head, broad shoulders slumped forward, engaging his back muscles and sending heat through my body.

I wasn't sure. I would have to call the police, but I didn't want to do that without a story. My options were fading like the night.

"Calling it in. I've wasted enough time on you," I decided reluctantly.

Damn shame about my phone. I was going to have to go and find a pay phone or borrow another one. What a pain.

"You know, hearing my curse might stop you from telling my story, but who knows what other story it could lead you to? It might be a bigger one?"

"Not possible, this is big." I added more of my magic to keep the bars holding him strong. Tiredness flooded me, and I knew I couldn't maintain the cage for much longer.

"You don't know, though. Besides, don't you want to help me?"

It was possible he had something to tell me about his curse that would lead to a bigger story. I glanced at him, avoiding his privates with difficulty. He was strong, fit, confident, and not at all like someone who needed help.

"No risk, no gain," he prompted.

The way he stared at me as if he was seeing into my soul like there was a connection forming between us. I immediately looked away. I couldn't let something like that happen.

"But if you were cursed, then surely you've done something wrong." He lowered his eyes, and it was obvious I had something on him. "Something you need to atone for, then?"

"And I am. But if you call the police and I get locked up, then I can't continue my atonement." His expression pleaded with me, and my heart weakened.

"Not my problem." I had to remain strong.

"Look, you have to believe me." He reached out to me, his arm carefully in the gap between the bars.

I stepped back, my shoes splashing in the puddles on the concrete floor. I couldn't get involved with this man, this werewolf, on any level. I'd made a mistake coming here.

"Someone tipped you off because I was out here seeing things I shouldn't."

"More like the other way around. You were ready to kill when I arrived."

"Only because I had a job to follow a client's wife…" He withdrew his arm and ran it through his messy hair.

"Oh, I see, like that is it?"

"No, I have to take what work I can get on account of the curse."

"Stop using the curse as an excuse."

"Just listen for a moment to what I have to say," he gritted out, clenching his fists, and stopped short of banging them into the bars. It was good to know the spell was keeping him from getting to me.

I held my breath, biting back words to spit at him. If my phone weren't damaged, I'd have called the police by now. I was wasting my time here and putting myself in danger. I needed to leave, but something held me back each time I considered it. Perhaps it was the glimmer in his eyes, a softness, or the glimpse of honesty in his face.

Even though the rest of my logical brain screamed at me that he would kill me without thought in his wolf form, my feet stayed firmly planted.

"By following Celine, I ended up at The Whispering Tome. This hadn't been part of the plan for the evening…"

Now, he had my attention. He'd been to *that* bookstore. Hell, it might be my lucky night, and he knows about the book I'd been trying to find all these years. I listened to him for a change, clenching my jaw so as not to interrupt.

"I saved her. Something was going down, and if you call it in, then I won't be able to keep Celine safe."

"When I got here, you were in no position to save her or anyone else," I noted. It was too easy to pick holes in his story. I had to know for sure he had something of value for me.

"Only because I left it too late, and the change happened because I'm cursed. But by staying, I helped her. There's something more going on here. Let me use my private investigation skills to find out, then how about I come to you with the story to print."

He had a tempting offer. But could I ever trust a wolf who was cursed? He'd done something in his past that would always haunt him and whoever was with him.

"Deal, but first, I need information on you. Tell me why you're cursed."

"Only if you do a blood promise."

I spied a window nearby, went over, and threw a brick in it, shattering the glass. Picking up a shard, I returned to the cage.

"Hold out your hand." I cut the edge of the glass into the end of my left pointer finger, blood pooling quickly. Then, I did the same to his finger.

I let my blood drip down on the ground, as did his, joining together, while I recited the promise.

This was the most stupid thing I'd ever done.

Yet I did it…

… because of him.

Chapter 4

Erik

I HATED WITCHES.

Yet, here I was, making a blood promise with one. The irony wasn't lost on me. I must have lost my mind agreeing to this. This witch, Mira, seemed hell-bent on destroying the miserable remnants of my life, and I was letting her.

Despite my better judgment, something about her drew me in. The way her hazel eyes flickered with intelligence and curiosity, the mischievous twitch of her lips when she smirked, and the way her long, deep red hair cascaded past her shoulders, framing her face like a fiery halo. And the curves of her body, accentuated by the tight leather pants and jacket she wore, didn't go unnoticed. She was unlike any witch I'd encountered before.

"So, spill it. What's the deal with your curse?" Mira demanded, her arms crossed over her chest, eyes boring into me as if she could see through my soul.

Fuck, I wish I had some clothes right about now.

"Gimme a sec, will ya? It's not like I go around telling this story every day." I needed a moment to gather my thoughts. Plus, I was still reeling from being caught in this damn cage.

This entire night had been one giant clusterfuck, and I was starting to doubt I'd ever see the light of day again.

"I was young and stupid, all right? There was this chick, Beatrix Blackfeather. Found her in the woods one night, meant to be out looking for the crew on a murder case, but there was fog so thick you could barely see your own hand in front of your face. She was doing some kind of ritual, and I knew it was bad news, but fuck, I couldn't look away."

I could still picture it like it was yesterday. The way the moonlight danced off her skin, the scent of the herbs she was burning, sweet and sickly all at once. The way her voice seemed to echo through the trees, ancient words I couldn't understand but felt in my bones.

"I should've stopped her, but I was too caught up in the moment. Let her seduce me, let her finish the ritual. And then all hell broke loose."

Mira's gasp cut through the air like a knife. Her red lips parted in shock. "Wait, you mean… Beatrix Blackfeather? The one who summoned the demon that terrorized Lycanridge for five days?"

I nodded, shame burning in my gut. "Yeah, that's the one. All those people who died… it's on me. I could've stopped it, but I didn't."

Mira took a step back, her eyes wide. The disgust was written all over her face, and I couldn't blame her. I disgusted myself most days.

"The head witch, Helena, found out about it when she was punishing Beatrix. Tracked me down and cursed me, forced me out of the pack, and made me leave everything I loved behind. Said I deserved to be alone forever, and she was right."

"Why doesn't anyone know about this?" Mira asked, her voice barely above a whisper.

"Part of the punishment. I'm supposed to suffer in silence, bear the weight of what I did alone. And I have for years now."

The words hung heavy between us, the truth of what I'd done laying bare for her to see. I braced myself for her reaction, for the moment when she'd turn away from me in disgust, just like everyone else had.

But instead, she stepped closer, her eyes searching mine. "That's a heavy burden to bear alone," she said softly, and for a moment, I thought I saw a flicker of understanding in her gaze.

I swallowed hard, my throat tight with emotion. "Yeah, well, I deserve it. I fucked up, and I have to live with the consequences."

We stood there in silence for a long moment, the weight of my confession hanging between us. For the first time in a long time, I didn't feel quite so alone. I'd take whatever company I could get, I suppose, even a fucking witch.

"You do deserve it. Smart of you to bind me in silence with a blood promise."

There it was, the response I always expected if I told a woman.

"Are you going to let me out then? So I can continue living my cursed life and try to bring some safety to those out there who need it. I need to go see if Celine made it home alive."

"And tell her husband so you can collect your fee?" I noted the disgust in her voice.

"Unless you're going to pay for my rent, then yes."

"Fine. But you're coming with me to The Whispering Tome. I want you to introduce me to the owner."

"Now, why does a lovely lady like yourself want to go to a bookstore like that?"

"None of your business."

It may well not be, but I could smell a secret she was hiding. She'd taken interest in the bookstore as soon as I'd mentioned it. And there was something else that had escaped me. Fuck it, with all this changing of forms and being caged and confessing like this, I was struggling to keep track of what was important.

"You going to let me out?"

Mira snapped her fingers, and like that, the magical bars faded. I hesitated. What if there was residual magic that had shot painful surges of electricity through me? No wonder my head was a fucked-up mess.

"It's gone, come on," she instructed, turning to march away from me.

"You're forgetting something."

She turned quickly and glared at me. "What?"

I gestured to my naked body, enjoying her glance lower to my dick. "I need clothes if you want to go to the bookstore with me."

Her cheeks flushed, and I enjoyed her discomfort. Low of me, I know, but hey, it was about as much fun as I could have since the curse.

"Don't you have spares or something?" she grumbled.

"Yeah, in my car." I looked up at the ceiling. Based on the gaps in the roof showing the brightening sky, I might not make it to my car without being seen. So far, I hadn't been cited for indecent exposure, and I wasn't about to make now the first time.

"So go there."

I cleared my throat and pointed upwards. "Without being seen?"

"How do you cope normally?"

"This isn't a normal situation for me… far from it."

"Well, you can't borrow mine."

"What a shame, on account of us being the same size and all," I answered, trying not to laugh.

"You are infuriating, you know." She pointed her finger at me.

I smiled back and bit my tongue so as not to inflame her further, though she was more beautiful when frustrated like this.

"Your car is closer, right?" I asked, taking a guess.

"Can't say I want you in my car."

"Fine then, I'll head off. Someone will report me, and your chance of going to The Whispering Tome is smoke." I strode forward, hating the feel of the dirty puddle water on my feet. Of all the places I'd been forced to change in over the years, this was the worst.

"Hang on, I might have some gym clothes or something in the car." She hurried to catch up to me.

"I don't know about putting on your clothes."

"Beggars can't be choosers."

"Right, true. Show me what you have." How I was ever going to show myself in public wearing her clothes, I wasn't sure. But all I needed to do was to get to her car, change, then to my car, change again, and then we would be right to get to the bookstore.

She got out her keys, and the Mazda ahead beeped. She opened the door, clambering in to grab something from the back seat. Then she shimmied out, turned to me, and threw me a plastic bag.

"Here, put these on."

"Turn around then. Give a man some privacy."

She rolled her eyes and turned, but not before I glimpsed a smile forming on her face. Dare I give myself some hope that I was piercing her tough exterior?

No, I told myself firmly as I took out black sweatpants and put them on. They were too short, coming up to mid-calf, and the fabric stretched so tightly across my thighs and hips that the seams popped in protest. I prayed they held long enough to change into my own clothes.

"They'll do," she said.

"Hey, you're not meant to be looking."

"Get the shirt on, and let's go to the bookstore."

"We should have breakfast, nothing fancy. It is too early for this sort of store to be open," I hurried after her, slipping a bright pink T-shirt over my head with the words 'Girl Power' on it. As I pulled the shirt down, her scent enveloped me, a captivating blend of vanilla and jasmine. It was intoxicating, and for a moment, I forgot about my ridiculous appearance, lost in the essence of her that clung to the fabric.

"No way, it wasn't that sort of a night," she retorted.

"You did see me naked, though…"

"Shut it, or I'll make up a story to publish about you."

She would too. Best I didn't push it further with her. I was about to walk off when I noticed something to the side. I couldn't believe my luck as I bent down and picked up my phone. And it had some charge and appeared to be working, the screen a little cracked in one corner. I shoved it into the pocket of the borrowed pants.

"Hurry up," Mira called out to me.

"Don't be so impatient," I called back, jogging up to her.

We walked silently down the road, weaving through the quiet streets toward the bookstore. The early morning air was crisp, and the city was just beginning to stir, with a few cars and pedestrians dotting the streets.

"Are we close, or are you taking me the wrong way?" she asked after a few minutes.

"Look, I don't think this is the right time of day to turn up to a bookstore like this. Tonight would be better. Plus, just ahead is my car. I need to change. If anyone saw me like this, I would get reported. I'd be better off wearing nothing."

"I have to get to the bookstore."

I had made up my mind that as soon as I saw my car, I'd point to the bookstore, then change out of these ridiculous clothes. I wasn't wrong in thinking they would be enough to cause someone to ring the police.

As we turned into the street, a heavy feeling sunk in my belly. In the distance, I heard the wail of police sirens growing louder. My instincts were screaming at me that something was wrong. I quickened my pace, Mira matching my stride, her brows furrowed in concern.

We were just a block away from the bookstore when a police car rushed past us, its lights flashing and siren blaring. It screeched to a halt in front of The Whispering Tome, where several other police cars were already parked. Officers were rushing in and out of the store, their faces grim and purposeful.

"What is going on?" Mira started to run toward the bookstore, her voice laced with worry.

Every fiber of my being was telling me to turn around and walk away. The last thing I needed was to get involved with the police, especially in my current state. But as I watched Mira's retreating figure, a protective instinct kicked in. Against all my better judgment, I raced after her.

What the fuck had happened last night?

Chapter 5

Erik

THE STENCH of death hit me like a punch to the gut, my wolf senses lingering from my recent transformation as I approached The Whispering Tome. More police sirens wailed in the distance, their piercing sound cutting through the early morning air.

The flashing lights of the patrol cars cast an eerie red and blue glow on the bookstore's façade, creating a surreal, almost nightmarish scene. I fought the urge to turn and run, my bare feet slapping against the cold, rough pavement as I hurried to keep up with Mira.

My heart sank when I saw the yellow crime

scene tape cordoning off the area, fluttering in the breeze like a warning flag. Mira marched up to the nearest officer, her press badge already in hand, while I hung back, acutely aware of my ridiculous appearance in her ill-fitting gym clothes and my bare feet. The damp ground sent a chill through my soles, and I could feel the curious stares of onlookers boring into my back.

"What's going on here?" Mira demanded, her voice carrying an air of authority that commanded attention.

The officer, a young man with a tight-lipped expression, glanced at her badge before responding, his voice strained. "The owner, Alistair Moreau, was found dead inside earlier this morning."

Mira's eyes widened, her voice tinged with shock and excitement that sent a shiver down my spine. "Dead? Was it murder?"

The officer hesitated, his jaw clenching as he clearly weighed how much he should reveal. The tension in the air was palpable, and I could sense the unease radiating from him. "We're still investigating, but it appears to be a homicide. That's all I can say for now."

But Mira wasn't one to give up easily. She leaned in closer, her eyes locking with the officer's, her gaze intense and unwavering. "I'm sure you can tell me a little more, Officer," she purred, her voice dropping to a conspiratorial whisper that seemed to hang in the air between them. "Off the record, of course."

I watched in amazement as the officer's resolve seemed to falter under Mira's scrutiny, his shoulders sagging almost imperceptibly. If I had tried that, dressed as I was, I'd probably be in the back of a squad car by now, the cold metal of the handcuffs biting into my wrists.

"I can't, and you know that, Mira," the officer said, but there was a hint of uncertainty in his voice, a slight tremor that betrayed his internal struggle.

Mira pouted her lip, her eyes widened in a look of innocent pleading I knew was carefully calculated. "Who knows? I might have something that could help, but I won't know if you don't tell me."

The officer sighed, glancing around to make sure no one was within earshot. The sound of his breath was heavy, weighted with the burden of his decision. "Fine. But you didn't hear this from me…"

As he began to speak, his voice low and urgent, I marveled at Mira's ability to extract information. She was a force to be reckoned with, a master manipulator who knew just which strings to pull. I found myself grateful that she was on my side, at least for now. She really could've ruined the little life I had left, exposed my curse to the world, and left me with nothing. It meant something to me that she didn't, but I tried not to put any weight on it. I'd been alone for so long now, trusting only myself. I couldn't risk trusting another person, no matter how compelling they might be.

I took a moment to survey the scene, my eyes roaming over the gathered crowd and bustling officers. Despite my disheveled appearance, no one seemed to be paying me any attention. The officers were too focused on securing the area and keeping curious onlookers at bay, their voices raised in sharp commands and warnings.

A sudden thought struck me. This could be my chance to do some investigating of my own, to uncover the truth behind Alistair's murder and the dark forces at work in Lycanridge.

I glanced at Mira, still engrossed in conversation with the officer, her brow furrowed in concentration. I made my decision, moving as casually as possible toward the entrance of The Whispering Tome. My heart pounded as I ducked under the crime scene tape, the flimsy barrier offering little resistance. It was a bold move, even for me, but I couldn't ignore the nagging sense that there was more to this case than met the eye. Celine needed my help, and I'd be damned if I let her down. Plus, there was the matter of my paycheck from Marcus. I needed that money to keep myself afloat, to maintain the fragile illusion of normalcy I had built for myself.

Inside, the bookstore was eerily quiet, the usual hustle and bustle of customers replaced by an oppressive silence. The musty scent of old books was overshadowed by the coppery tang of blood, the smell so thick I could almost taste it on my tongue. I swallowed hard, steeling myself for what I might find. If I could uncover something useful, maybe I could take it to Marcus and collect my pay for helping Celine. It was a long shot, but I had to try.

As I picked my way through the cluttered shelves, the books looming over me like silent sentinels, the feeling of being watched lingered. The hair on the back of my neck stood on end, and I found myself wishing I had something more substantial than Mira's gym clothes to protect me. But there was no turning back now. I had a task to do and was determined to see it through, no matter the cost.

If I were being honest with myself, there was another reason I was so determined to investigate on my own. Mira. I couldn't explain it, but something about her made me want to impress her, to prove my worth. Maybe it was her quick wit or her fearless approach to journalism. Or maybe it was the way she looked at me like she could see past the curse and scars of the person I used to be. The person I still hoped I could be again.

I stepped deeper into the bookstore, and the signs of a struggle became increasingly apparent. Bookshelves had been knocked over, their contents scattered across the floor in a chaotic mess. It looked as though a tornado had torn through the place, leaving a trail of destruction in its wake. I carefully navigated the debris, my bare feet picking a path through the sea of books, the rough edges of the pages scraping against my skin.

A strange scent hung in the air, growing stronger as I approached the back of the store. It was an oddly sweet aroma, like pears and mint, completely out of place in the musty confines of The Whispering Tome. The possibility that it was somehow connected to Alistair's death nagged at me, a clue I needed to unravel.

As I turned the corner, my breath caught in my throat. There, lying in a pool of blood, was Alistair Moreau. His lifeless eyes stared up at the ceiling, his face frozen in an expression of terror that made my blood run cold. But it was what surrounded his body that sent a chill down my spine, a sickening sense of dread settling in the pit of my stomach.

Symbols had been drawn on the floor in blood, their jagged lines and curves forming a complex pattern around Alistair's corpse. A large pentagram dominated the center of the design, its five points connected by a circle of intricate runes. At each point of the pentagram, a different symbol was inscribed—a crescent moon, a stylized eye, a serpent devouring its tail, a crossed pair of daggers, and a twisted sigil I couldn't quite make out.

Surrounding the pentagram were other symbols I recognized from when I first saw the witch in the woods practicing a magic she shouldn't. Was this what the murder was about? Was someone trying to bring back the black magic? My blood chilled, and my breath shortened, the air suddenly seeming thin and inadequate. If they were, I had to stop them this time, no matter the cost.

A hexagram, also known as a witch's star, was etched in blood to the left of Alistair's body. Its six points were interwoven with more unknown runes. The overall effect was one of dark, ancient energy, a palpable sense of malevolence that seemed to radiate from the symbols. I could almost feel the power pulsing from them as if they were alive, imbued with a sinister purpose.

I forced myself to look closer, scanning the area for any clues that might help explain what had happened. That's when I noticed something wedged under a nearby bookshelf as if it had been kicked there during the struggle. I crouched down and reached for it, my fingers closing around the smooth leather cover of a book.

As I pulled it out, I realized the pages were crumpled and stained with what looked like blood, the once pristine paper now marred with evidence of violence. My heart raced as I realized the significance of my discovery. This book was the key to unraveling the mystery of Alistair's murder, a vital piece of the puzzle.

As I tucked the book into the waistband of my borrowed gym pants, the elastic digging into my skin, a twinge of guilt surfaced. I knew I should turn it over to the police, but something held me back, a powerful instinct I couldn't ignore. Maybe it was my selfish desire to solve the case and collect my paycheck from Marcus to prove my worth. Or maybe it was the fear of what might happen if the book fell into the wrong hands, the terrible knowledge it contained unleashed upon the world.

But there was another reason I hesitated, one I

didn't want to admit to myself. I wanted to show Mira I was more than just a cursed werewolf and could be a valuable ally in this fight against the dark forces that threatened Lycanridge. It was foolish to seek her approval, but I found myself drawn to her like a moth to a flame.

I took a deep breath, trying to calm my racing thoughts and focus on the task at hand. I had to find a way to keep the book safe and figure out my next move. But even as I tried to push aside my doubts and fears, the feeling I was in over my head persisted, a nagging sense that I was being pulled into a web of darkness and deceit from which I might never escape.

The symbols on the floor seemed to mock me, their jagged lines and curves a reminder of the dark magic that had cursed me so long ago. I had thought I had escaped that world, but now it seemed to be pulling me back in, dragging me toward a fate I couldn't control, a destiny I had never asked for.

I straightened, the book securely hidden in my waistband, the weight of it a constant reminder of the burden I now carried. I knew I had to get out of here before someone spotted me and the police or the killer realized what I had found.

I took one last look at Alistair's body, a sense of

dread settling over me like a heavy shroud. I had a feeling this was only the beginning, and the dark forces at work in Lycanridge were just getting started. But I was determined to see this through, to uncover the truth and stop whoever was behind this madness, no matter what it cost me.

As I turned to leave, I suddenly found myself face to face with Officer Chen, his expression one of surprise and suspicion. "Hey! What are you doing back here?" he demanded, his hand instinctively reaching for his weapon.

I froze, my mind racing as I tried to come up with an excuse. I couldn't tell him the truth, but I needed to think of something fast before he grew even more suspicious.

"I was just looking for the restroom," I lied, trying to sound as casual as possible.

"As if I haven't heard of that excuse before. I'm taking you in for questioning."

Oh, fuck. Now I'd done it. No need to be worried Mira might turn me in. I'd gone and blundered straight into trouble all by myself, and just after I'd found the book Celine had mentioned last night.

Had she returned? That was risky if she had. This was one mystery that was burning through me to solve.

I straightened my shoulders, causing the tight pink top to ride up and expose my somewhat toned belly. Not a good look in this situation. "You'd be wasting your time, Officer Chen."

"Are you going to make this the hard way?" His grip tightened on my shoulder as he steered me toward the exit.

I suppose I should be glad he hadn't recognized me. Maybe these ridiculous clothes were helpful after all. But then there was the book tucked in the back of my pants. How would I ditch it before being shoved into the police car?

I felt a bead of sweat trickle down my back, and my heart pounded in my chest. I knew I had to think fast to come up with a lie that would satisfy his curiosity without arousing further suspicion.

"Officer, wait!" Mira's voice rang out, her footsteps echoing on the hardwood floor as she approached.

The officer paused, turning to face her with a scowl. "Miss, this is an active crime scene. You can't be in here."

Mira flashed her press badge, a confident smile on her face. "I understand that, Officer. But this man is with me. He's my photographer."

The officer's eyes flicked from Mira to me, his

brow furrowed in confusion. "Your photographer? Dressed like that?"

Mira didn't miss a beat. "We were at the gym when we heard about the murder. There wasn't time to change."

I held my breath, waiting for the officer to call her bluff. To my surprise, he hesitated, his grip on my shoulder loosening slightly.

"Fine," he said, at last, his voice gruff. "But don't touch anything. And if I catch either of you interfering with the investigation, you'll both be spending the night in a cell."

With that, he released me and stalked off to confer with his colleagues. I let out a shaky breath, my heart pounding as I turned to face Mira. Clearly, she had used her magic to persuade the officer we could stay.

I rubbed my shoulder where the officer's fingers had dug in, wincing at the lingering ache. "Thanks," I muttered, my gratitude genuine despite the discomfort. "I owe you one."

Mira waved off my thanks with a dismissive gesture, her keen eyes already scanning the crime scene, taking in every detail. She turned to me, her gaze sharp and probing. "You can start by telling me what the hell you've stuffed down your... my pants."

A smirk tugged at my lips. *Damn, she's good,* I thought to myself. "You should've been a detective."

"Not the first time I've heard that." She held out her hand, palm up, expectantly. "The book?"

I hesitated, my mind racing to find a way to keep the book to myself. It needed to be destroyed, but I couldn't do that if I handed it over to Mira. "Shouldn't we look around first?" I asked, hoping to stall.

Mira's eyes narrowed, a dark, stormy look that caused my skin to shiver and my wolf to push back. I wasn't used to being talked to this way, but I had to admit, I sort of liked it. Better than being alone, which I was accustomed to. "Haven't you done that already? The book?" she demanded, her tone leaving no room for argument.

I shifted my weight, feeling the rough fabric of her gym pants against my skin. "No. I needed to make sure Celine is all right."

"That's right, the wife of the man who hired you or something." Mira crossed her arms over her chest, her stance unyielding. "I need it for more important reasons."

"Like what?"

"I don't have to tell you."

"You do. I'm the one with the book."

Mira rolled her eyes, a huff of frustration

escaping her lips. She tapped a finger on her arm, the rhythm betraying her impatience. I could feel her frustration radiating out with a heat I hungered for. "Used to working alone, huh?"

I met her gaze, a challenge in my eyes. "I bet you are used to working alone."

"How about we mix things up and work together instead of independently?" a cheeky smile tugging at the corner of her mouth.

"Why would we do this?" I asked.

"Because I'll wager that whatever is happening here is something bigger than either of us. We'll be stronger together."

Since I was beginning to like her company, I was willing to give this a go. "But why would you want to work with me? I'm cursed."

Her response took my breath away. "Because everyone deserves a second chance." She meant it. I could tell. But I didn't think I was worthy of another chance, only atonement.

I held out my hand, a peace offering. "Fine, only because it will help the people of Lycanridge."

She took my hand in hers, her grip firm. "For the people of Lycanridge." The warmth from her palm extended out, and for a moment, I was flooded with images that took my breath away.

Then her touch was gone, and I was left alone again, an emptiness within awakened.

Her expression was serious. "Fine, hand over the book," she demanded again.

I glanced around, lowering my voice to a hiss. "Not here. Besides, don't you want to look at the body? It's surrounded by symbols."

Her eyes widened, curiosity and concern warring on her face. "What do you mean?"

I shrugged, feigning indifference. "If you can stomach it."

Mira pushed past me, carefully stepping around the scattered books on the floor. I heard her gasp, the sound confirmed my fears this was the sort of magic that had gotten me cursed in the first place.

"This brings up too much of my past," I murmured, my voice heavy with the weight of my curse and the secrets I so desperately wanted to keep hidden.

Mira turned to face me, a determined set to her jaw. "We need to stop whoever is doing this."

I nodded, relieved we were on the same page. "I'm glad we agree on that point."

She shook her head, then surveyed the scene once more, taking in the symbols. I quickly pulled my phone out and hoped the battery held, snapping a few photos, making sure to capture the intricate details of the symbols.

"So, how do we stop them?" she asked, turning to me, a fear in her eyes that chilled my blood.

I swallowed hard, the gravity of the situation settling on my shoulders. "You don't know how? You're a witch..."

"This is more powerful than me..."

"Good thing we're in this together now." I glanced around the store, taking in the mess of books, the dead body, and the symbols that made me sick to see. It wasn't one detail in particular, but all of them together. "How about we go and question Celine at the museum? I overheard her last night saying she knew where the book was, and now the owner is dead."

Mira frowned, her brow furrowed in thought. "Why didn't they take the book?"

"It had slipped out of sight." A twist of luck, I thought. "Maybe they were interrupted."

"They might not be the only people wanting the book?"

"No," I said softly, the weight of our task settling heavily on my shoulders. How would we work out who wanted to practice such dangerous magic? More importantly, how would we stop them?

Chapter 6

Erik

THE MORNING SUN'S harsh glare assaulted my eyes as I stumbled out of the bookstore, my mind reeling from the gruesome scene I'd just witnessed. The symbols, the blood, the lifeless eyes of Alistair Moreau—it was all too much to process. I desperately needed a drink, or maybe a whole bottle, to numb the rising panic that threatened to consume me.

As if on cue, my phone buzzed insistently in my pocket, jolting me back to reality. With shaking hands, I fumbled for it, my heart pounding as I saw Marcus's name flashing on the screen.

"Erik, what the hell is going on?" Marcus

demanded, his voice laced with panic and frustration. "I've been trying to reach Celine for hours, and she's not answering her phone. Please tell me you have some information on her whereabouts."

I swallowed hard, my mouth suddenly as dry as the Sahara. How could I tell Marcus that his wife was tangled up in something far more sinister than a simple disappearance? That the very fabric of our reality was being threatened by an ancient evil?

"Marcus, listen," I began, my voice rough and strained, guilt weighing heavily on my shoulders. "I will do everything in my power to find Celine."

"She was always going on about magic and shit," grumbled Marcus, panic edging into his voice. "As if she could do it herself if she met with this man."

My pulse quickened, thumping hard against my ribcage. "What man?"

"How should I know? The one she was fucking. You should know all of this." His tone heightened, accusation and desperation mingling in his words.

I felt a surge of guilt wash over me, knowing I had let Marcus down. A simple job of following Celine had turned into a nightmarish pursuit of ancient secrets and dark magic.

"Marcus, trust me, I will find her," I said, my

voice barely above a whisper. "Could she be at the museum right now?"

"Yes, but she's not answering. No one is answering the phones there." Marcus sighed heavily, the weight of the world pressing down on him.

That was odd. Surely, someone would answer the phones, especially at the reception desk. An uneasy feeling settled in the pit of my stomach as I realized I had to get there quickly.

"I'll go there now," I promised, glancing up at Mira who waited nearby. Her presence was a reassuring constant in the chaos that surrounded us.

"Just… just keep me in the loop, Erik. Please."

"I will, Marcus. I swear it."

As I ended the call, Mira's hand found my shoulder, her touch warm and reassuring. "We'll figure this out, Erik," she said, her voice soft but determined. "To the museum, then?"

I looked into her eyes, seeing the same fear and uncertainty I felt reflected back at me. But there was something else there, too—a glimmer of hope and a spark of defiance that refused to be extinguished.

"Let's go," I said, my voice determined despite the panic rising within.

As Mira wove through the streets of Lycanridge, the feeling we were racing against the clock grew stronger with each passing moment. Every minute we wasted seemed to bring us closer to the edge of an abyss from which there might be no return.

I gripped the door handle, my knuckles turning white as Mira took a sharp turn, tires screeching against the asphalt. "Jesus, Mira!" I yelped, my heart pounding in my chest. "You trying to kill us before we even get to the museum?"

Mira shot me a sidelong glance, her eyes glinting with mischief. "Oh, come on, Erik. Live a little! Besides, I thought you werewolves were all about the thrill of the chase."

I snorted, shaking my head. "Yeah, well, usually I'm the one doing the chasing, not being chased by a madwoman behind the wheel."

Mira laughed, the sound cutting through the tension that had settled over us like a fog. "You're just jealous of my superior driving skills, wolf boy."

I rolled my eyes, but a smile tugged at my lips despite my best efforts. "Superior? More like terrifying. I'm pretty sure you just broke every traffic law known to man."

"Hey, desperate times call for desperate measures," Mira quipped, her voice growing serious. "We don't have time to waste, Erik. Celine's life could be on the line."

I sobered at that, the gravity of the situation

crashing over me like a tidal wave. She was right. Every second counted, and if Mira's driving could get us to the Lycanridge Museum of History and Antiquities faster, then I'd just have to hold on for dear life and pray to whatever gods were listening.

"What about you make good use of this time and see if you can find anything that can help us in the book?" Mira suggested, taking a left-hand turn way too fast.

"You'll need to slow down a bit if you want me to do that." I ignored her sideward glance and took out the book.

I allowed the book to fan open, and it was as if the words hit me straight away.

"When all seems lost and darkness reigns, speak these words to break their chains. 'By the power of the ancient light, I banish thee from mortal sight. Your curse is broken, your power undone, by the strength of the moon and the rising sun,' " I read aloud.

"Sounds like a sort of curse breaker," Mira replied, stepping on the pedal to go faster as she ran a red light.

"Can't say I feel my curse is broken." I braced myself, thinking another car was going to hit us for sure in the intersection.

"Not for you."

"For who, then?"

"I don't know. But how about you remember those words? Who knows if they might be helpful?"

"I'll commit them to memory. Anything that could give us an edge." Which wasn't going to be easy to do with her driving, but I had to do something. I couldn't live with myself if I didn't stop the dark magic from being used this time.

The Lycanridge Museum of History and Antiquities loomed ahead of us, its towering spires and Gothic architecture casting long shadows in the morning light. An eerie stillness hung in the air, a stark contrast to the usual bustle of visitors and staff.

As we climbed out of the car, the crunch of gravel beneath our feet echoed in the silence. I scanned our surroundings, my senses on high alert, the hair on the back of my neck standing on end.

Something caught my eye as we made our way toward the entrance. I froze, my blood running cold. There, etched into the sidewalk, was a symbol. The same symbol we had found at the crime scene, the one that had been haunting my dreams. I swallowed hard, a sense of dread settling in my stomach like a lead weight.

"Mira," I called out, my voice hoarse. "Look at this."

She hurried over, and as her eyes fell upon the symbol, a sharp gasp escaped her lips, echoing my shock and disbelief. "What the hell?" Her voice trembled, a mixture of fear and confusion. "These symbols… they're used in rituals meant for soul transference… when someone wants to switch bodies with another person."

Mira's words hung heavy in the air, the implications of her revelation sending a chill down my spine. The thought of someone forcibly removing a soul from its rightful vessel only to inhabit it with their essence was a violation of the highest order, a perversion of the natural order that made my stomach churn.

"Are you sure?" I asked, my voice barely above a whisper, as if speaking the words too loudly might somehow make them more real.

Mira nodded, her eyes still fixed on the symbol, a mix of revulsion and fascination playing across her features. "I've seen them before in some of the ancient texts I've studied. They're not exactly common knowledge, but…" She trailed off, her brow furrowed in thought.

I swallowed hard, my mind racing with the possibilities and implications of what we had stumbled upon. *If someone had indeed performed a soul transference ritual, if they had stolen another's body for their own purposes*—the thought was almost too horrifying to contemplate.

"What kind of person would do something like this?" I asked, my voice hoarse with emotion. "What could possibly drive someone to such lengths?"

Mira shook her head, her expression grim. "Power, most likely. The ability to cheat death, to live on in a new form… it's a temptation some might find too strong to resist."

I shook my head, my mind racing, trying to make sense of the impossible. "This symbol, those at the bookstore… it's all connected somehow."

Mira opened her mouth to respond but was interrupted by a sudden chime from her phone. She frowned, pulling it out of her pocket. "That's weird," she muttered. "My phone hasn't been working since I dropped it."

Her face paled, and her eyes widened as she read the message. "Look at this," she whispered, her voice barely audible.

I leaned over her shoulder, my heart pounding as I read the words out loud on the screen.

"Turn back now, before it's too late. The truth will only bring pain and suffering. You have been warned."

A chill ran down my spine, a sense of foreboding washing over me. "Who sent this, Mira?" I asked, my voice low and urgent.

She shook her head, her eyes filled with a haunted look I knew all too well. "I don't know. It's from an unknown number."

I took a deep breath, trying to calm my racing thoughts. "Mira, what aren't you telling me? What do you know about all of this?"

She hesitated, her eyes filling with tears. "My mother," she whispered, her voice breaking. "She was killed by the black magic, Erik. I... I've been trying to stop it ever since to make sure no one else has to suffer like she did."

I felt a surge of sympathy wash over me, and I reached out, taking her hand in mine, her skin soft and warm against my calloused palm. "I'm so sorry, Mira. I had no idea."

She wiped away her tears, her jaw set with determination. "That's why we have to keep going, Erik. We have to find out the truth, no matter the cost."

I nodded, my resolve strengthening, pushing aside the fear that threatened to consume me. "You're right. Let's go."

We rushed inside the museum, our footsteps echoing off the marble floors, the sound amplified by the eerie silence that engulfed the building. The musty smell of old artifacts and the faint hint of cleaning products hung in the air, a stark reminder of the secrets that lay hidden within these walls.

"Where is everyone?" Mira whispered, her voice tinged with unease.

I shook my head, my senses on high alert, every fiber of my being screaming that something was wrong. "I don't know, but something's not right."

As we made our way through the exhibits, our eyes scanning for any sign of Celine or the hooded figure, a sliver of light spilling out from a slightly ajar door caught my attention. I motioned for Mira to follow me, and we crept toward the door, our hearts pounding in unison, the sound echoing in my ears. With a trembling hand, I pushed it open, steeling myself for what lay beyond.

The sight that greeted us stopped me dead in my tracks, my blood turning to ice in my veins. There, sprawled on the floor, was Celine. Her lifeless eyes stared up at the ceiling, her body surrounded by a pool of blood, the coppery scent overwhelming my senses. And standing over her, cloaked in swirling tendrils of dark magic, was a hooded figure.

Time seemed to slow to a crawl as the figure turned toward us, its face obscured by shadows. I felt Mira's hand grip my arm, her nails digging into my skin, a reminder I wasn't alone in this nightmare.

And then, as quickly as it had appeared, the figure vanished, leaving us alone with the horror of what we had just witnessed, the weight of our failure pressing down on us like a crushing burden.

Chapter 7

Erik

THE WORLD around me shattered into a million pieces as I stared at Celine's lifeless body, the hooded figure's dark magic still swirling in the air. Hot and unrelenting rage surged through my veins, propelling me forward. I couldn't let this monster escape, not after what they'd done.

Without a second thought, I sprinted after the hooded figure, my heart pounding in my ears as I navigated the museum's twisting halls. The figure was fast, their movements fluid and almost super-natural, but I was determined to catch them.

I pushed myself harder. My werewolf speed and agility gave me an advantage as I closed the distance between us. The exhibits blurred past me, with ancient artifacts and priceless treasures reduced to a hazy backdrop in my single-minded pursuit.

Just as I was about to reach out and grab the figure, they vanished around a corner. I skidded to a halt, my eyes scanning the area for any sign of where they might have gone.

Fuck, it was as if they'd vanished. Gone, poof, no trace they were even here. How was I going to return to Mira with nothing? Then I noticed something glinting on the floor.

I crouched down, my fingers closing around a strange amulet. It was unlike anything I had ever seen before. The metal twisted and warped into a symbol that made my skin crawl. It was cold to the touch, the metal seeming to leach the warmth from my skin.

With the amulet clutched tightly in my hand, I returned to Mira, my mind racing with questions. She was kneeling beside Celine's body, her eyes red-rimmed and her face pale.

"They got away," I said, my voice rough with anger and frustration. "But I found this." I held out the amulet, watching as Mira's eyes widened in recognition.

She took it from me, turning it over in her

hands. "I've seen this symbol before," she murmured, her voice distant. "In my mother's research. She was studying it before she… was murdered."

I felt a chill run down my spine, a sense of unease settling in the pit of my stomach. "What does it mean?"

She shook her head, her brow furrowed in concentration. "It's connected somehow to the black magic that killed her. And now Celine. That's all I really know."

Her voice broke, and I placed a hand on her shoulder. "We'll figure this out," I said, my voice firm with conviction. "We'll find out who's behind this and stop them. I promise."

Mira nodded, her jaw set with determination. "I know, Erik. I just… I can't lose anyone else to this darkness."

I met her gaze, my eyes fierce with resolve. "You won't."

I needed to end the darkness that threatened to consume us all, not just for Mira's sake but for my own as well. The urge to help and protect her from the same fate that had befallen her mother and now Celine was overwhelming. It was a feeling I hadn't experienced in a long time, a sense of purpose that had been missing from my life ever since my curse had taken hold.

For years, I had struggled with the weight of my curse and the fear I would lose control and hurt someone during one of my full-moon episodes. It had left me feeling isolated and alone, convinced that I was a monster unworthy of love or companionship. But standing there with Mira, seeing the determination in her eyes and the trust she placed in me despite my affliction, I realized that perhaps I wasn't as lost as I'd thought.

Helping Mira, fighting alongside her to uncover the truth and stop the spread of this dark magic, felt like a chance at redemption. It was a chance to prove to myself that I was more than just a creature ruled by instinct and bloodlust. It was a glimmer of hope in the darkness that had consumed me for so long, and I clung to it.

Sirens wailed in the distance, their urgent cries piercing the stillness of the museum. We'd run out of time. I turned to Mira, ready to suggest we get out of there when the sound of footsteps echoed through the museum. The steps were heavy and purposeful, the kind that demanded attention and promised trouble.

My heart sank as I recognized the familiar figure of Officer Chen, his face set in a grim expression that spoke volumes about his intentions.

He strode toward us, his eyes fixed on the lifeless body of Celine that lay at our feet. His gaze flickered to me, and I saw the accusation in his eyes, the certainty I was somehow responsible for this tragedy.

"I should have known I'd find you here, standing over another body," he said, his voice dripping with disdain.

I felt my hackles rise at the insinuation in his tone. "I had nothing to do with Celine's death," I growled out, my fingers tightening around the amulet.

Officer Chen's eyes narrowed, his gaze flicking to the claw marks that marred Celine's lifeless form. "The evidence suggests otherwise," he said, his voice dripping with disdain. "You're a werewolf, after all. It's in your nature to kill."

I opened my mouth to protest, but Mira stepped forward, her eyes blazing with anger. "That's ridiculous," she snapped, her voice ringing out in the stillness of the museum. "Erik was with me the entire time. He couldn't have done this."

Officer Chen's gaze shifted to Mira, his expression skeptical. "And why should I believe you? For all I know, you could be covering for him."

Mira met his gaze unflinchingly, her chin lifting in defiance. "Because I'm telling the truth. Erik is innocent, and if you'd bother to look past your prejudice, you'd see that."

Officer Chen's jaw tightened, but he didn't argue further. "This isn't over," he said, his voice low and menacing. "I'll be watching you, Nolan. One false move, and I'll have you behind bars before you can blink."

With that, he ushered us out of the room, leaving us standing in the reception area, making it clear we weren't to reenter it.

I let out a shaky breath, my heart pounding in my chest.

"Thank you again," I said softly, meeting Mira's gaze. "For standing up for me."

"I can't lose my number one partner in solving this case," she responded, her words filled with a sincerity that caught me off guard.

Her comment sent a surge of warmth through my chest, a feeling of validation and belonging I hadn't experienced in longer than I could remember. It wasn't just the acknowledgment of my usefulness, though, that certainly played a part. It was the underlying sentiment, the unspoken affirmation I was more than just a cursed werewolf, more than a mere tool to be used and discarded.

She turned it over in her palm, her fingers tracing the intricate patterns and symbols etched into its surface. "Erik, look at this," Mira said, holding up the amulet to the light. "These symbols have to mean something."

I leaned in closer, her brow furrowed in concentration as I studied the amulet. "You're right," I murmured. "And I think I've seen them before in the museum's exhibit on ancient occult artifacts."

Without another word, she turned on her heel and strode toward the exhibit, leaving me no choice but to follow. As we entered the dimly lit room, an unease washed over me. The artifacts on display were old, their surfaces worn and tarnished with age, and yet there was something about them that felt almost alive, like they were watching us from behind their glass cases.

Mira moved from one display to another, her eyes scanning the symbols and markings on each artifact, until she stopped in front of a small, nondescript case tucked away in a corner of the room. "Here," she said, her voice barely above a whisper. "The symbols on this case match the ones on the amulet."

I moved closer, my eyes widening as I saw the intricate pattern of lines and curves etched into the surface of the case. It was an exact match to the amulet in my hand.

"What do you think it means?" I asked, my voice low and urgent.

Mira shook her head, her eyes never leaving the case. "I'm not sure, but I have a feeling it's important."

"What if the amulet is connected to the artifacts in the museum, ones that might be helpful to those practicing the dark magic?"

"Then we better find them."

"Where do we start?" There were five levels of artifacts in this museum.

"Maybe the amulet will help us." She held out her hand, the amber pendant in her palm.

"Hmm…" She held it up and moved it around, moving forward to the entrance of the museum. It glowed. "This way." There was obvious excitement in her voice.

Together, we made our way deeper into the museum, the amulet clutched tightly in my hand. I had no idea what we would find, but I knew whatever it was, it would bring us one step closer to the truth behind the dark magic that had brought us here.

Then she suddenly stopped, and my pulse quickened. She reached out, her fingers brushing against the symbols on the wall. She placed the amulet in a small hole, and suddenly, there was a loud clicking sound. The wall behind the case shuddered and then began to move, revealing a hidden door that had been concealed behind it.

"A secret room," Mira breathed out, her voice filled with awe.

This was it, my chance to avenge Celine's death. To help her husband say goodbye, but more importantly, it was my chance to right my past. And this time, I wasn't going to fuck it up.

I stepped forward and took out the amulet, my heart pounding as I raised it to the door. As soon as it made contact, there was a blinding flash of light, and the door swung open, revealing a small, dimly lit room beyond.

Chapter 8

Mira

THE DOOR CLOSED BEHIND US, sending a shiver down my spine. The air in the hidden room was stale and heavy, as if it had been sealed away for centuries. My eyes slowly adjusted to the dim light that seemed to emanate from the very walls.

"What is this place?" I whispered, my voice sounding too loud in the oppressive silence.

Erik shook his head, his gaze sweeping over the shelves and tables that lined the room. "Whatever it is, Celine was doing some serious research here."

I stepped forward, my heart pounding as I took in the sight before me. The shelves were filled with ancient books and scrolls, their pages yellowed and brittle with age. On the tables, I saw scattered notes and journals.

With trembling fingers, I reached for one of the journals laid out on the heavy wooden table pushed up against the wall, my breath catching in my throat as I read the words on the first page. "The dark magic that plagues Lycanridge… I believe I have found its source." A chill settled over me. "She knew about the dark magic," I breathed out. "She wanted to be part of it, but she was human."

"Why?" Erik moved to stand beside me, his warmth soothing in this cold room.

I flipped through the pages, my heart racing as I scanned Celine's notes. "She outlines how it could help her wield magic." I shook my head. This was wrong, and worse, it would never work. Right? A human could never use magic. It just wasn't possible.

"I didn't think that was possible." Erik poked around the room, knocking over a pot of ink.

"Not this way. Whoever this person is lied to her." I glared at him. He should know better.

"This would bring back black magic."

"Yes. I must say she was thorough with her research. She mentions an ancient cult that once operated in the area," I said, my voice shaking slightly. "They used amulets like the one we found to track and locate their members."

Erik's eyes widened, and he reached for the amulet. "You mean this thing could lead us to the hooded figure?"

I nodded, a thrill of excitement and fear coursing through me. "Celine's notes indicate the amulets are connected to the cult's dark magic. If the hooded figure is using that same magic…"

"… then the amulet should react to it," Erik finished my sentence.

"It should."

"Yes, it's the breakthrough we needed." In his excitement, he turned to me, grabbed my shoulders, and kissed me on the lips. The heat exploded in my mouth, and my breath hitched. The kiss deepened ever so slightly, both of us wanting more. Then suddenly, we came to our senses and pulled away.

"Let's go," he said, his face red, unable to meet my eyes.

"Not so quick. I want to read some more." I turned to the journals, wanting a moment to compose myself. A simple kiss had left me rattled with desire coursing through me out of control. How could he have me reacting like this?

"Fine. I'll do some of my own then." Erik

continued to flick through the pages of a nearby book.

"Don't like researching?" I asked, raising an eyebrow.

"No, more of a hands-on investigator," he replied, his eyes never leaving the pages.

"Good thing we've teamed up then."

He grunted in response, clearly focused on his task. He flipped through several more pages, his brow furrowed in concentration until suddenly, he stopped.

"The symbols, they're here again," he remarked, his voice carrying a tone of intrigue and anticipation.

"No way." I moved to lean over his shoulder, my curiosity piqued.

There, on the yellowed pages of the ancient tome, were the same symbols we had seen on the amulet and in the secret room. The intricate lines and curves seemed to dance before my eyes, forming a beautiful and unsettling pattern.

"It says here these symbols are part of an ancient language used by a cult that practiced dark magic centuries ago," Erik said, his finger tracing the faded text. "The cult believed the symbols held power and could be used to summon and control dark forces."

I felt a chill run down my spine at his words. "And the amulet? What does it say about that?"

Erik flipped to another page, his eyes scanning the text. "The amulet was a key, a way to unlock the power of the symbols. It says the cult used it in their rituals to focus their magic and bend it to their will."

"So, whoever killed Celine and my mother, they must have been using the amulet and the symbols to control the dark magic," I noted, the pieces starting to fall into place in my mind.

"Exactly," Erik replied, his eyes meeting mine.

"We need to be careful," I said, my voice low and serious. "If we're right about this, then we're not just dealing with a killer, but with an entire cult wanting to connect to dark magic."

Erik's jaw tightened, his eyes hardening with resolve. "Times like this, I wish I could call for backup."

I took a deep breath, the weight of our mission settling on my shoulders, and old grief tightened around my chest. "What can a witch and a were-wolf do?"

"Stop them." His words sent shivers over my skin.

I nodded, my mind racing as I tried to make

sense of it all. "But why now? What do they hope to gain?"

"It's my fault," Eric said.

"How do you reason that?"

"If I hadn't stopped Beatrix all those years ago, then there wouldn't be any witches out there hungry for this type of magic."

"But witches know about this magic, and from what I'm reading, this hooded figure is hungry enough for it. I mean, it's not like you were the one who inspired Beatrix to use the dark magic, were you?"

"No. But I didn't stop her."

"And you are paying for it. Come on, help me by reading these notes. We need as much information as we can get."

Erik grumbled and sidled closer to me. For a moment, it was hard to concentrate, but then I refocused. As I pored over Celine's research, my mind kept circling back to Erik's curse.

It would be difficult to break a witch's curse. In the past, I wouldn't even try, but as I scanned the pages, I found myself hoping to find something that would break his curse. I don't know why, but it seemed to me he'd paid his dues.

The ancient book spoke of a malevolent force that had held sway over Lycanridge for centuries, a dark power that granted its wielder immortality and dominion over the town's supernatural inhabitants. This power was apparently the source of the dark magic that now plagued our community, and it was intimately connected to the curse that afflicted Erik.

I felt a thrill of excitement as the pieces began to fall into place. If we could unravel the mysteries of this ancient power, we might find a way to break his curse. But more than that, we might be able to uncover the deeper truths that lay at the heart of Lycanridge's supernatural world, truths that had been hidden for far too long.

A particular passage caught my eye. It described an ancient spell, one that had been placed on Lycanridge centuries ago by the cult leader himself. The spell was designed to grant the cult leader immortality and power over the town's supernatural inhabitants, bending them to his will.

A chill ran down my spine as I read the words, my mind racing with the implications. Someone was trying to tap into its power to claim the cult leader's twisted legacy for themselves. To be immortal. But as I studied the passage more closely, I realized the spell was not unbreakable. Celine had discovered a way to weaken its hold, to sever the ties that bound Lycanridge's supernatural community to the cult leader's will.

My heart raced with possibility as I turned to Erik, my eyes shining with newfound hope. "There's a spell," I breathed out, my voice trembling with anticipation. "It's the key to everything." Erik's brow furrowed in confusion, but I couldn't contain my enthusiasm. "Don't you see? If we can break the spell, we can free Lycanridge from the cult leader's influence. We can stop the hooded figure and put an end to the dark magic once and for all."

"But how do we break it?" he asked, his voice low and urgent.

I turned back to Celine's notes, scanning the pages for any clue or hint. And then I saw it. A single line that made my heart skip a beat. "The spell can only be broken by one who carries the blood of the cult leader," I read aloud, my voice barely above a whisper.

Erik's eyes widened, and I could see the realization hitting him just as it had hit me. "The hooded figure," he murmured, his voice grim. "They must be a descendant of the cult leader."

I nodded, my mind racing with the possibilities. I knew it wouldn't be easy. The cult leader's descendant would be powerful, steeped in the same dark magic that had terrorized the town for centuries.

As I closed the ancient book, I felt a sense of

purpose settle over me. There was a way forward emerging. Timing was now everything.

I turned to Erik, my eyes blazing with determination. "We have to find the hooded figure," I stated, my voice steady and sure. "We have to break the curse and end this once and for all."

The amulet on the table between us began to glow, its surface pulsing with an eerie red light. We froze, our eyes locked on the ancient artifact.

"It's reacting to the dark magic," I whispered, my voice trembling. "The hooded figure must be close."

Erik's hand closed around the amulet, his eyes blazing with determination. "Then let's not waste any more time. We have to stop them before they can hurt anyone else."

I took a deep breath, steeling myself for what lay ahead. We had come too far to turn back now, and the stakes had never been higher. The fate of Lycanridge, and perhaps the entire world, rested on our shoulders.

We raced out of the hidden room, following the pulsing light of the amulet that grew stronger with every step, leading us deeper into the heart of the town. With the dark magic in the air, a weight pressed down on my chest, but I refused to let it stop me. We had come too far to turn back now.

I would stop this hooded figure and avenge my mother's death, no matter what.

Chapter 9

Erik

THE HOODED FIGURE'S dark magic was like a tangible presence in the air, growing stronger with every step we took. The amulet guided us, the light we needed in such dark times. My heart pounded hard, a mixture of fear and anticipation coursing through my veins. We were close. I could feel it.

Mira's revelation about the connection between my curse and the ancient power that held Lycan-ridge in its grip had only strengthened my resolve. I had lived with this curse for so long and had come to accept it as an inevitable part of my existence. But now, faced with the possibility of a cure, I felt a fierce determination burning within me.

We turned down a narrow alleyway. The amulet's light pulsed with a sudden, blinding intensity. I stumbled to a halt, my eyes widening as I took in the sight before us.

At the end of the alley stood an old, dilapidated building, its windows boarded up and its walls covered in a thick layer of grime. But it was what lay beyond the building that caught my attention.

A circle of hooded figures stood in the building's small courtyard, their voices raised in an eerie chant that sent shivers down my spine. The air around them crackled with dark energy, and I could feel the amulet's power surging in response.

"Umm... so which one is the hooded figure we're looking for?" I asked, trying to ignore the urge to run. If only I had the ability to change into a wolf right now, I might have the confidence to stay and fight. Fuck this curse.

"A witch's coven," Mira breathed, her voice barely audible over the pounding of my heart. "They must be trying to tap into the dark magic. They're part of the cult. I'm sure of it."

I nodded, my grip tightening on the amulet. "Then let's stop them," I said grimly. "If they succeed, there's no telling what kind of chaos they could unleash."

Mira's hand found mine, and we crept

forward, using the shadows to conceal our approach. But as we drew closer to the coven, I felt a sudden, sickening surge of power wash over me.

"Intruders!" one of them hissed, her voice sharp and venomous. "They carry the amulet of the ancients. They must be stopped!"

The coven turned as one, their eyes glinting with malice beneath their hoods. Mira tensed beside me, her hand reaching out and her magic flowing out.

"We don't want to fight you," I called out, my voice steady despite the fear that gripped me. "We only want to find the one who has been using the dark magic to terrorize Lycanridge."

But the witches only laughed, a harsh, grating sound that set my teeth on edge. "You are too late, *wolf.*" One of them sneered. "They are already aware of your presence. They will come for you, and when they do, you will beg for the sweet release of death."

With a wave of their hands, the witches unleashed a barrage of dark energy that sent Mira and me flying backward. I hit the ground hard, my breath knocked from my lungs. Beside me, Mira struggled to her feet, her magic fading from her hands as if it was drained away.

"We have to get out of here," she gasped, her voice tight with pain. "We can't take them all on at once."

I nodded, staggering to my feet. The amulet's glow had dimmed, but I could still feel its power thrumming through my veins. We had to keep moving, had to stay one step ahead of the hooded figure and the dark magic.

As we fled the coven's courtyard, I could hear the witches' laughter ringing in my ears, their taunts and threats echoing through the night. But I refused to let them shake me. We had come too far to turn back now, and I knew whatever lay ahead, we would face it together.

The amulet's light pulsed with renewed intensity as we raced through the streets, guiding us to the hooded figure. Their dark magic set my teeth on edge and made my skin crawl. But we couldn't turn back now, not when we were so close to the truth.

But I pushed on, my resolve hardening with every step. We were now so close I could almost taste the hooded figure's fear in the air. They knew we were coming and knew we would stop at nothing to put an end to their reign of terror.

As we rounded the final corner, the amulet's light flared with a blinding intensity, and a grim smile tugged at the corners of my mouth. The hooded figure may have had the power of dark magic on their side, but they had underestimated the strength of our determination, and the depth of our love for Lycanridge.

Chapter 10

Erik

MIRA and I raced through the streets of Lycanridge, our footsteps echoing off the cobblestones. As we turned down a narrow side street, the amulet's light flared brighter, casting eerie shadows on the walls around us.

Suddenly, the street opened up before us, revealing a gaping hole in the ground. I exchanged a glance with Mira, my heart pounding in excitement. We were getting closer. I could feel it. I pulled up short, my breath catching in my throat as I realized where we were.

The entrance to Lycanridge's abandoned underground rail network loomed before us, a dark, yawning maw that seemed to swallow the amulet's light. "They're down there," Mira whispered, her voice tense. "I can feel it."

I nodded, my grip tightening on the amulet. Whatever secrets lay buried beneath Lycanridge's streets, we would uncover them together.

With a deep breath, I stepped forward into the darkness, Mira close behind me. The amulet's glow was our only guide as we descended into the depths of the old railway tunnels, our footsteps echoing off the damp stone walls.

The air grew colder as we pressed on, and I could feel the weight of the earth above us, pressing down like a physical force. But still, we followed the amulet's light, winding our way deeper and deeper into the labyrinth of tunnels.

And then, just when I thought we might be lost forever in the darkness, the amulet flared with a sudden, blinding intensity. I stumbled to a halt, my eyes straining to see through the blinding glow.

There, at the end of the tunnel, stood the hooded figure, their dark robe billowing in an unseen breeze. They turned to face us, their features obscured by the deep cowl of their hood.

"So," they said, their voice a rasping whisper that sent shivers down my spine. "You have come at last, wolf boy and his little mate."

I growled, my fingers curling into fists at my sides. "We know what you've been doing," I said, my voice low and dangerous. "The dark magic, the curses, the murders. It ends now."

The hooded figure laughed, a harsh, grating sound that echoed off the tunnel walls. "You know nothing," they sneered. "You think you can stop me? I have been planning this for centuries, waiting for the right moment to strike."

Mira stepped forward, her silver magic dagger glinting in the amulet's light. "We know about the cult," she said, her voice steady and sure. "We know about the curse that has held Lycanridge in its grip for so long. And we know you are the key to breaking it."

The hooded figure stiffened, and for a moment, I thought I saw a flicker of fear in the shadows beneath their hood. But then they threw back their head and laughed, a sound that chilled me to the bone.

"Fools," they hissed. "You think you can break the curse? I have lived for centuries, feeding off the dark magic that flows through this town's veins. And now, with the amulet's power, I will be unstoppable."

They raised their hand, and I felt the amulet's power surge in response, a searing heat that burned through my veins. But Mira was faster, her dagger flashing through the air to bury itself in the hooded figure's chest.

The figure stumbled back, a gurgling cry escaping their lips. And then, as we watched in horror, their hood fell back, revealing a face that was all too familiar.

"Celine," Mira gasped, her eyes wide with shock. "But how? We saw you die."

The woman who had once been Celine smiled a twisted, cruel thing that held no warmth. "Death is just another curse," she rasped, her voice barely human. "One that I have long since broken. I've crossed over to the supernatural side, and I'll have no one stop me."

I stared at Celine, my mind reeling. How was this even possible? What dark magic had allowed her to cheat death itself?

This was my time to right my past.

She lunged forward, her fingers curling into claws, but I was ready for her. I could feel the strength of the wolf coursing through my veins, fueling my determination to fight back. With a cry of defiance, I met her assault head-on, my fists clenched and my eyes blazing with resolve.

We collided in a flurry of blows, our bodies slamming against each other as we grappled for dominance. I could feel the impact of her strikes, the bruising force behind each hit, but I refused to yield and let her gain the upper hand.

Drawing upon every ounce of my training, every hard-earned lesson in combat and survival, I countered her attacks with fierce precision, my movements fluid and instinctive. It was a dance of sorts, a brutal ballet of clashing wills and desperate measures.

With a swift kick, I managed to sweep her legs out from under her, sending her crashing to the damp stone floor of the tunnel. But even as she fell, she lashed out, her claws raking across my arm, drawing blood and eliciting a hiss of pain from my lips.

I stumbled back, my hand pressed against the wound, but I didn't have time to dwell on the injury. She was already recovering, springing to her feet with an agility that belied her human form.

Our eyes locked—a silent acknowledgment passing between us. This was a fight to the death, a struggle for survival in which only one of us would emerge victorious. As we circled each other, our breaths coming in ragged gasps, I knew I would stop at nothing to ensure I was the one left standing when the dust settled.

With a final, primal roar, I charged forward, my

fists raised and my heart pounding with the thrill of the battle. And as we clashed once more, the echoes of our struggle reverberated through the underground depths.

But even as we fought, I could feel the amulet's power waning, its light flickering and dimming. Celine's laughter rang in my ears, a mocking reminder of the curse that still held me in its grip.

And then, just when I thought all hope was lost, Mira was there, her silver magic swirling, flashing in the darkness. Her magic surged forward, and I realized the time had come to speak the ancient words that would break the curse.

"When all seems lost and darkness reigns, speak these words to break their chains. 'By the power of the ancient light, I banish thee from mortal sight. Your curse is broken, your power undone, by the strength of the moon and the rising sun.'"

With a final, desperate cry, Mira buried her magic deep in Celine's heart, and the world exploded in a blinding flash of light. When the glare faded, Celine was gone, her body crumbling to dust before our eyes. The amulet lay shattered on the ground, its power spent at last.

I staggered to my feet, my breath coming in ragged gasps. Mira was beside me, her face streaked with blood and grime but her eyes shining with a fierce, unwavering light. "Is it over?" she asked, her voice barely a whisper.

"It's over," I said, my voice rough with emotion. "Lycanridge is free from dark magic."

"Thanks to you."

"I couldn't have done this without your help. We make a good team."

A small smile tugged at the corners of Mira's lips. "Celine didn't stand a chance with us on the case."

I nodded, a lump forming in my throat as I looked at her. "Your mother would've been proud…" I couldn't finish the sentence, my voice trailing off as I saw the mist of tears in Mira's eyes.

Without a word, I pulled her into a tight embrace, feeling the weight of the past slowly lifting from our shoulders.

Chapter 11

Mira

"BUT WHAT ABOUT YOUR CURSE?" I asked, my voice soft as we stood in the quiet streets of Lycanridge.

A deep sorrow crossed over Erik's face. "I don't matter…"

I placed a finger on his lips to stop him talking. "Don't say that," I whispered, my heart aching for him. "You matter to me more than anything."

The weight of Celine's research bore down on me, the revelation that Erik's curse was no ordinary affliction but an ancient and powerful spell that held the key to unraveling the deeper mysteries of

Lycanridge's supernatural world. Breaking it wasn't just about freeing Erik from the shackles of his monthly transformations, it was about unlocking the secrets that had been buried for far too long and the truth that could change everything we thought we knew.

"We'll find a way to break your curse," I vowed, my gaze unwavering as it met his. "Together, we'll uncover the truth behind Lycanridge's supernatural past and liberate you from this burden once and for all."

Erik nodded, his expression a mix of determination and apprehension. "I know we will. But even if we do, I'm not sure if I'll feel any different. This curse... it's been a part of me for so long, I can't imagine my life without it."

His words struck a chord within me, a reminder of the profound impact the curse had had on his existence. It wasn't just a physical transformation he endured each month but a fundamental part of his identity, a defining aspect of who he was.

As if to punctuate his point, Erik reached up and touched the broken amulet that hung around his neck, the once-powerful artifact now nothing more than a shattered remnant of its former self. The moment his fingers brushed against the jagged edges, a flicker of realization crossed his face, a dawning understanding that sent a shiver down my spine.

"It's gone," he whispered, his voice barely audible over the pounding of my heart. "The curse... I can't feel it anymore. It's like a weight has been lifted, a shadow that's no longer cast over my soul."

I stepped closer, my hand reaching out to touch the broken amulet, a tangible confirmation of the momentous change that had occurred. The curse was indeed broken, and the ancient magic that had held Erik in its grasp for so long finally dissipated into the ether.

But even as relief washed over me, a sense of uncertainty lingered, a question mark hovering over what this newfound freedom might mean for Erik, our mission, and the future of Lycanridge itself.

"How do you feel?" I asked, my voice soft, almost hesitant.

Erik's gaze softened, and he pulled me into his arms, holding me tight against his chest. "I don't know what I did to deserve you," he murmured, his voice thick with emotion.

We stayed like that for a long moment, drawing strength from each other's presence. And then, with a deep breath, we turned to face the town that had been our home for so long.

Lycanridge had changed in the wake of Celine's defeat. The dark magic that had once hung heavy in the air was gone, replaced by a sense of warmth and light I had never felt before. Supernaturals and humans alike walked the streets openly, no longer hiding in the shadows.

But there was still work to be done. The delicate balance between the supernatural world and the human one was fragile, easily upset by fear and misunderstanding. It would take time and effort to maintain the peace we had fought so hard for.

As Erik and I walked hand in hand through the town square, I couldn't help but feel a sense of hope for the future. We had faced so much together—Erik's curse and the dark magic that had threatened to consume us all—and we had emerged stronger for it.

A sense of pride and accomplishment washed over me. The town that had once been torn apart by fear and mistrust was now a place where supernaturals and humans could coexist peacefully, working together to maintain the delicate balance we had fought so hard for.

Erik's hand tightened around mine, and I

looked up to see a mischievous glint in his eyes. "Come on, let's get something to eat," he said, his voice filled with a newfound lightness.

A grin spread across my face, a surge of affection for the man beside me filling my heart. But as I glanced down at his attire, a chuckle escaped my lips. "Hang on, there's one thing you need to do first," I said, tugging at the pink top he was wearing.

"What's that?" he asked, feigning innocence.

"Get out of my clothes." I laughed, poking him playfully in the chest.

He winked at me, his lips curving into a smirk. "Only if you help me."

I rolled my eyes, shaking my head in amusement. "Typical guy, only thinking of one thing." Despite my teasing tone, I couldn't deny my thoughts were drifting in a similar direction.

Erik leaned in close, his breath tickling my ear as he whispered, "Easy to do when I'm around you."

I laughed, feeling a shiver run down my spine at his proximity. "I'm not that easy," I countered, meeting his gaze with a challenging stare.

"I'll be the judge of that," he murmured, his eyes filled with a heat that made my heart race.

A sudden gust of wind caught my attention. A single, weathered page from an ancient book fluttered to the ground at our feet. Curious, I picked it up and gasped as I read the faded inscription.

"What is it?" Erik asked, his brow furrowed with concern.

"It's a clue," I whispered, my heart racing with excitement and trepidation.

"The shadows whisper, they call forth the wolf, he is drawn by the Beacon."

Erik's eyes widened, a flicker of recognition and apprehension crossing his features. "Who is the Beacon?"

I shook my head, my mind spinning with possibilities. "No idea. But surely you're the wolf?"

He nodded slowly, his gaze locked on mine. "Then you must be the Beacon."

A shiver ran down my spine at the thought, a sense of destiny settling over me like a heavy cloak. "Whatever it is, this is a mystery that literally is calling us."

Erik pulled me closer, his strong arms encircling me as he pressed a fierce kiss to my forehead. "Then let's not waste any time," he said, his voice filled with determination.

I nodded, folding the page carefully and tucking it into my pocket.

Our journey was far from over, but one thing was certain. The future of Lycanridge was ours to shape, and we would stop at nothing to protect the town and the people we loved.

Look out for more stories from Ruby Fox coming soon!

Bk1: Homecoming, Haunted Heirloom, and Hexes

About the Author

Ruby Fox loves writing cozy paranormal mysteries, especially set in Australia where she lives. Bought up on Murder She Wrote, and Midsommer Murders, it was a natural step to write cozy mysteries, and then add in paranormal element to mix things up.

Acknowledgments

Heartfelt thanks to my dog, Sprinkles, for keeping me company during my writing sessions, and to my incredible editors, Kaylene and Nikki, for their invaluable help in polishing this story.